The Big Hat

W9-CCQ-899

by Bobby Lynn Maslen
pictures by John R. Maslen

Scholastic Inc.
New York • Toronto • London • Auckland • Sydney • Mexico City • New Delhi • Hong Kong • Buenos Aires

Available Bob Books®:

Set 1: Beginning Readers

Set 2: Advancing Beginners

Set 3: Word Families

Set 4: Compound Words

Set 5: Long Vowels

Ask for Bob Books at your local bookstore, or visit www.bobbooks.com.

No part of this publication may be reproduced, stored in a retrieval system, or transmitted in any form or by any means, electronic, mechanical, photocopying, recording, or otherwise, without written permission of the publisher. For information regarding permission, write to Scholastic Inc., Attention: Permissions Department, 557 Broadway, New York, NY 10012.

ISBN 0-439-14503-1

6 5 4 3 2   6 7 8 9 10 11/0

Printed in China
This edition first printing, May 2006

Tex was
a big man.

Tex had
a big hat.

Max was a cat.

Max was in the big hat.

Rex was a big dog.

Rex sat on the hat.

Rex sat on Max.

"Get off, Rex!"

Max was mad at Rex.

Tex was mad at Rex.

Rex got up.

Max was OK.
Rex was OK.
Tex was OK.

The End

List of 23 words in <u>The Big Hat</u>

Short Vowels

<u>Aa</u>	<u>Ee</u>	<u>Ii</u>	<u>Oo</u>	<u>Uu</u>	sight
at	end	big	dog	up	a
cat	get	in	got		OK
had	Rex		off		the
hat	Tex		on		was
mad					
man					
Max					
sat					